IF I COULD SWIM

For information , please contact author:
Andy Hair
andy@mrhairphysed.com
www.mrhairphysed.com

Copyright ©2021

How to use this book

 **Active Reading & Colouring Book**

Read the book aloud, to a class or to another person.

Personalize the pictures that are printed white by colouring them in

*At the end of the book create a list of ways you can use the action.

ENJOY YOUR SWIMMING BUT
REMEMBER TO ALWAYS HAVE
SOMEONE WATCHING YOU
WHEN YOU ARE IN AND AROUND
WATER.

I really want to learn to swim
but the town I live in has
no pool, no river, no lake
and no beach to practise in.

My PE teacher is amazing though. She showed us how to swim at school using different equipment. She called it 'Dry Land Swimming'.

It's not the same but it's still lots of fun.

When I was young my family and I moved towns. We moved from the outback to the coast.

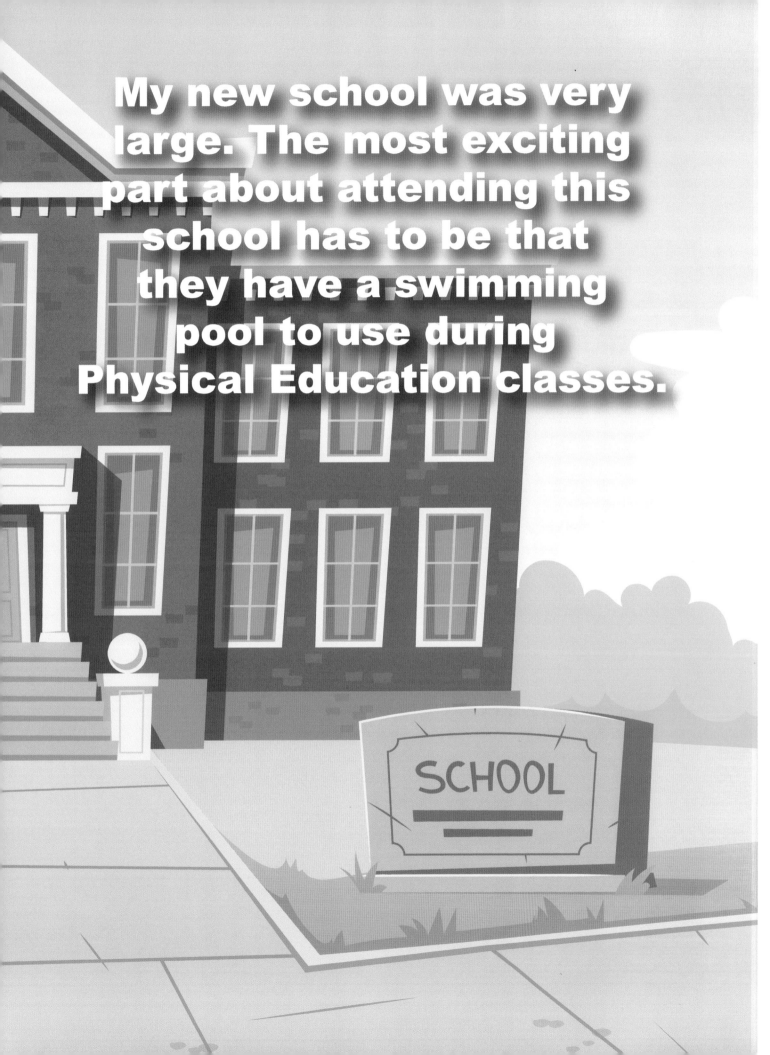

My new school was very large. The most exciting part about attending this school has to be that they have a swimming pool to use during Physical Education classes.

In Physical Education we learn how to swim.

I told my new teacher that I learnt how to swim at my last school on a skateboard.

I went up and down the pool almost 1000 times it felt like.

After a few lessons at my new school, my Physical Education teacher asked me if I would be interested in swimming for the school.

Of course, I said 'YES'!

Swimming for the school was so much fun. I loved it so much that I started to train with the team before school to get stronger.

When I started to swim really well I was allowed to swim at the lake.

But still I wanted to get better so I kept training really hard.

Lap after lap after lap.

I entered a swim race
against other swimmers
in my town.

Although I didn't win I
had a lot of fun.

I kept training but this time it was before and after school.

My teacher thought I would get really tired. But I had so much energy.

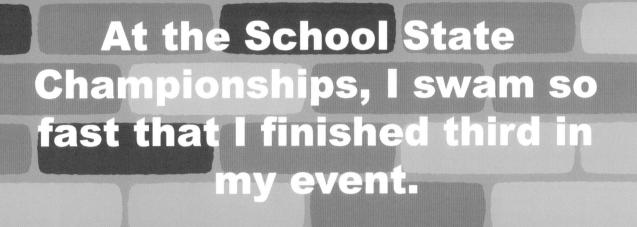

At the School State Championships, I swam so fast that I finished third in my event.

I even won this...........

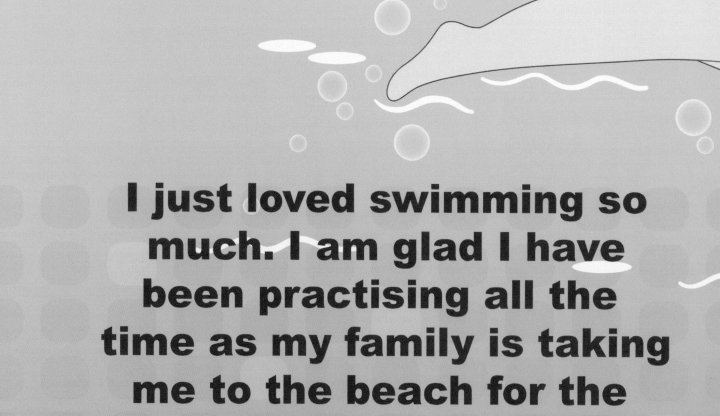

I just loved swimming so much. I am glad I have been practising all the time as my family is taking me to the beach for the first time.

I have heard that the
waves can be pretty scary
at the beach.

Arriving at the beach I could hear the waves crashing and could smell the ocean. It was beautiful.

I must admit though. The waves are big and I am a bit nervous about swimming in the ocean.

All of a sudden I was in trouble. The other swimmers around me were also in trouble. We were being pulled out to sea.

I tried to swim into the beach but the ocean was too strong. I was going further and further out. I was very scared.

I remember my swimming
training and what to do
when you get into trouble.

I raise my hand and wave
to the beach to try
and get the attention
of the lifeguards.

The lifeguard saves me.

Back on the beach the lifeguard talks to me about swimming at the beach and reminds me that the safest part of the beach is always between the red and yellow flags.

I was telling my swimming teacher about the beach. They decided that it was time to teach me about open water swimming and how to be safe in the water.

My family and I went on a holiday to a tropical island.

It was so warm and smelt like coconuts.

AQUAPA

I love the waterslides.

I love the beach.

On one of the days my family and I visited a tropical island.

My family hired snorkles and flippers so we could swim in the ocean and see what was under the water.

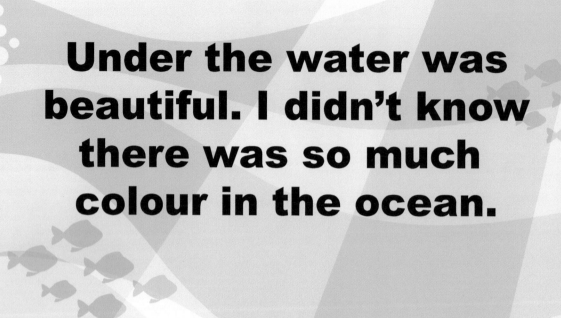

Under the water was beautiful. I didn't know there was so much colour in the ocean.

There are so many fish under the sea. I really like the orange fish. They are called clown fish.

Diving down deep I was able
to see the awesome coral.

I had to hold my breath for a long time to get down that far.

The stingrays are gorgeous
and very large as they swim
around me.

I can't believe it. My favourite animal in the world is the green turtle and it is swimming right in front of me.

I watch as the turtle raises it's head above the surface of the water to take a breath.

As soon as the turtle took a breath it turned and swam back to the ocean floor to feed on the sea grass.

I couldn't swim with the turtle as I can't hold my breath the same way a turtle can.

Back on the beach, my family and I shared stories about what we saw under the water. I told them all about the green turtle.

It was an amazing day.

In the hotel room I thanked my parents for helping to teach me how to swim.

If I did not know how to swim then I would not have been able to see my favourite animal swimming in the ocean.

I will always keep learning
how to get better at swimming.

Seeing a green turtle was pretty cool and I wonder what adventures I can do with my swimming when I get bigger.

Maybe one day I will swim around my country.

Until then though it's time to just swim and have fun.

Where can
you swim?

Draw
or write
your
answer

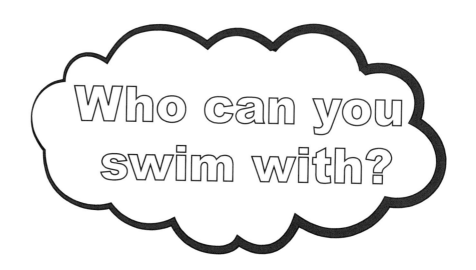

Who can you swim with?

Draw or write your answer

What would
you like to see
when you swim?

Draw
or write
your
answer

About The Author

Known for my high energy and youthful personality, I am a Physical Education and Movement Coach based in Geelong, Australia. My goals in life are to see students excel, achieve their dreams, have confidence and enjoy everything they do. My PE motto is DREAM, BELIEVE, ACHIEVE.

I live an extremley active life. I am passionate about endurance pursuits, pushing myself to my limit every single day. I am known for my high energy and passion in life and find my excitement around like minded and active people. My life's experiences have shaped how I wake up and see the world everyday. I embrace life and face it head on.

My legacy as an educator is to see children lead a healthy and active lifestyle, being the best they can be and reaching as far as they can with what they are given. It is my view that every child I teach is a world champion and together we have to discover which world champion they are.

Andy

Love this book? Scan the below code or head to:

www.mrhairphysed.com/books
to grab the latest
additions to the active library

Printed in Great Britain
by Amazon